Our SPECiAL World

World

MY
BODY

Liz Lennon

Contents

Franklin Watts
Published in Great Britain in 2018 by
The Watts Publishing Group

Copyright © The Watts Publishing Group, 2016

All rights reserved.

Series Editor: Sarah Peutrill
Consultant: Karina Philip
Cover Designer: Cathryn Gilbert

Editor: Sarah Ridley
Designer: Will Dawes

ISBN: 978 1 4451 4895 3
Printed in China

Franklin Watts
An imprint of
Hachette Children's Group
Part of The Watts Publishing Group
Carmelite House
50 Victoria Embankment
London EC4Y 0DZ

An Hachette UK Company
www.hachette.co.uk
www.franklinwatts.co.uk

FSC
www.fsc.org
MIX
Paper from
responsible sources
FSC® C104740

Picture credits: Alamy:- Disability Images: 8tl; Distinctive Images: 9t, 24bl; Image Source Plus: 7; Stephen Jones: 21; Myrleen Pearson: 11bl. Getty Images:- Tetra Images: 20. Photofusion:- John Birdsall: 19t, 24c; Tim Jones Photography: 9br. Shutterstock:- Mikkel Bigandt: 12; Boltenkoff: 13bc; Jacek Chabraszewski: 13c, 24tr; Hung Chung Chi: 15; DeeMPhotography: front cover cl; dotshock: 13cl; Alexander Ermolaev:11br; JM Gelpi: 18b, 24tl; Glovatskiy: 13tr; gorillaimages: 9bl; kiza54500: 10b; Denis Kuvaev: 5, 11t, 24tc; LooksLikeLisa: 14, 24br; Lopolo: 4, 22t, 22b, 23t; Robyn Mackenzie: 13bl; Nattika: 23c; oliveromg: 8b; karein oppe: front cover cr, 3b, 10t, 24cr; parinyabinsuk: 6, 24cl; Tinna Pong: 8tr; Rawpixel.com: front cover l; Mido Semsem: 3tl; Seregam: 13cr; Anastasia Shilova: 16, 24bc; Kuttelvaserova Stuchelova: 23b; Studio smile: 23cl; 3445128471: 3tr; topseller: 13tc; Fam Veld: 18t; wavebrealmedia: 17; wckiw: 1, 19b; Jaren Jai Wicklund: front cover cr; Wolna: 13tl.

Every attempt has been made to clear copyright. Should there be any inadvertent omission please apply to the publisher for rectification.

Amazing body

We all have a body. Our bodies
can do amazing things!

Jump

Think

Laugh

Body parts

Our bodies are made up of different parts. Each body part has a name.

Skin

Head

Hair

Neck

Arm

Shoulder

Hand

Finger

Knee

Leg

Toe

Foot

Can you match the words to the parts of this girl's face?

Eye   Hair   Nose

Mouth   Teeth   Chin

Do you know this rhyme?
Ten fingers,
Ten toes,
Two eyes,
And a little nose.

Bones and muscles

You have more than 200 bones in your body. Your bones and muscles are under your skin.

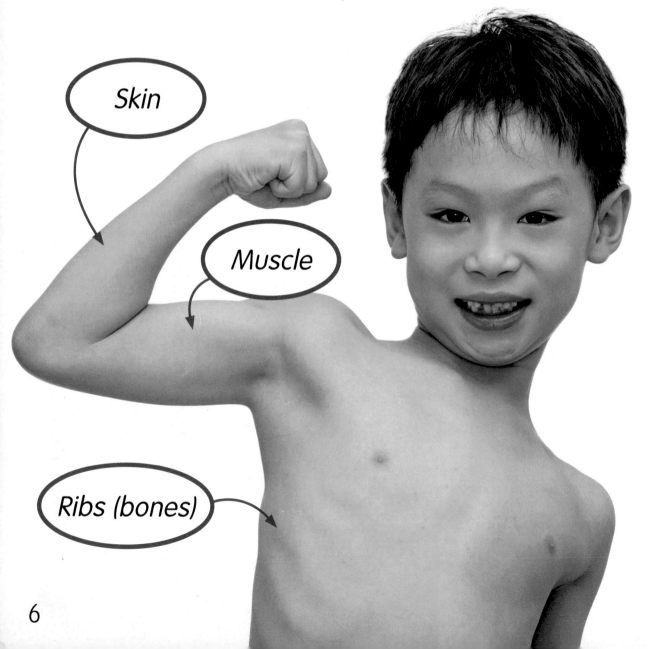

Skin

Muscle

Ribs (bones)

You have over 650 muscles in your body.

Kieran's muscles
lift his arms
to catch the ball.

Move your body!

Moving around is good for your body.
There are many ways to get moving.

Ride a bike

Swing from monkey bars

Run about

Go swimming

Play football

Go climbing

Which activities do you enjoy?

Amazing senses

We have five senses. They help us to find out about the world.

Seeing

Hearing

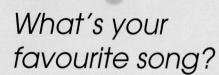

What's your favourite song?

Smelling

Tasting

Touching

Food and drink

Your body needs food and drink to stay alive.

Water is the best drink for your body.

Your body gets its energy from the food you eat.

Which of these foods do you like?

Keeping clean

Soap and water wash away dirt and germs.

It is important to wash your hands after you use the toilet and before you eat.

It is good to keep your body clean by taking baths or showers.

Daniel is washing his hair in the bath.

Do you prefer baths or showers?

Teeth

Max has learnt a song about brushing his teeth.

Brush, brush, brush your teeth, Gently to and fro, Up and down, round and round, Backwards and forwards we go.

We need to clean our teeth at least twice a day. This helps to keep our teeth healthy.

How else can you keep your teeth healthy?

Growing and learning

Our bodies change as we grow from a baby into an adult.

Oliver was once as small as his baby brother.

Jade's baby sister has learnt to sit up and stack blocks.

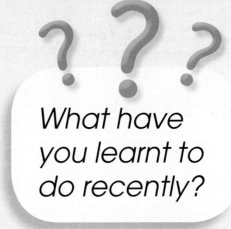

What have you learnt to do recently?

Tom is learning to read.

Ben wants to grow as tall as his brother.

Hurting yourself

Our bodies are good at healing.

Oliver has fallen over.
His mum cleans the graze
and puts a plaster on it.

Even broken bones mend.

It will take three or four weeks for my broken arm to heal.

All about me

Lily has made a book about herself.

Age: 5
Height: 108 cm
Eye colour: brown
Hair colour: black

Favourite activities: dancing, playing chase and swimming

Why don't you make a book about yourself?

Favourite photo: me and my twin sister

Favourite foods: cheese and strawberries

Favourite animal: hamster

Word bank

 Baby

 Face

 Food

 Muscle

 Reading

 Seeing

 Swimming

 Teeth

 Washing

Index